With great thanks to Laurence and Ljuba
For Alicia and her white bear
— S.P.

For Arthur and Zoé
— V.H.

Text © 2005 Svetlana Petrovic
Illustrations © 2005 Vincent Hardy
Published in 2009 by Eerdmans Books for Young Readers
an imprint of Wm. B. Eerdmans Publishing Co.

First published by Mijade in Belgium in 2005

Wm. B. Eerdmans Publishing Co.
2140 Oak Industrial Dr. NE, Grand Rapids, Michigan 49505
P.O. Box 163, Cambridge CB3 9PU U.K.

www.eerdmans.com/youngreaders

Printed in China

09 10 11 12 13 14   1 2 3 4 5 6 7

Library of Congress Cataloging-in-Publication Data

Petrovic, Svetlana, 1967-
Brown bear, white bear / by Svetlana Petrovic ;
illustrated by Vincent Hardy.
p. cm.
Summary: Alice likes the teddy bears she receives for
her birthday from each of her grandmothers, but soon
the bears are fighting for her attention.
ISBN 978-0-8028-5353-0 (alk. paper)
[1. Teddy bears — Fiction. 2. Grandmothers — Fiction.
3. Jealousy — Fiction. 4. Fighting (Psychology) — Fiction.]
I. Hardy, Vincent, ill. II. Title.
PZ7.P44725Bro 2009
[E]--dc22
                    2008046914

written by

Svetlana Petrovic

illustrated by

Vincent Hardy

Brown Bear, White Bear

Eerdmans Books for Young Readers

Grand Rapids, Michigan • Cambridge, U.K.

Alice got two teddy bears as gifts from her grandmas.
One bear was white, and the other was brown.

Except for their colors,
the bears were exactly the same.

The two grandmas had
always been good friends,
but soon they began to argue
about the bears.
"Alice likes the white bear better," said Grandma Jones.
"No, Alice likes the brown bear better," said Grandma Murphy.
"She'll take mine when she goes to sleep."
"No, she won't. She'll take mine."

Alice listened to their squabbles and smiled. The truth was,
she loved all bears: white, brown, and any other color.
But the bears — they didn't like each other.

Soon the bears began
to argue, too!

They argued during the day
when Alice was at school.

They argued at night
while Alice was sleeping.
They would both snuggle
up next to Alice, one on each
side, to see who could get closer.

Or they would pull on the blankets while Alice was asleep. First Alice was warm. Then she was cold. She would wake up in the middle of a battlefield.

When Alice was playing, she would make the bears sit side by side. The bears would push and kick each other. White Bear always ended up on the floor.

White Bear wanted to get even. He waited for the
right moment. Then he pushed Alice's school bag off
the desk and watched it land on Brown Bear's head.

One beautiful sunny day
Alice thought it would be nice
to have a picnic with the bears.

But White Bear took the mayonnaise and splattered Brown Bear with it. White Bear laughed until his sides hurt. Now he was the best looking bear — and the cleanest, too!

Brown Bear was angry. So he plopped grape jam on White Bear. Now it was Brown Bear's turn to laugh. White Bear was not only white — he was also purple!

Alice put the bears in the sink and washed off the mayonnaise and jam. Now she was angry.

"Enough is enough!" she said. "You two are really impossible!"

So Alice put White Bear in the closet.
And she set Brown Bear high up on the shelf.

"There! That should stop your fighting!" she said.

But Alice didn't know that White Bear was afraid of the dark. In the closet he began to sob. She also didn't know that Brown Bear was afraid of heights.

Up on the shelf Brown Bear
kept his eyes closed. He did
not dare to look down!

Finally, White Bear called
out to Brown Bear.
"Where are you?"

"I'm up here," Brown Bear
said. "I'm afraid of falling
down!"

"I wish I could help you," said White Bear, "but I'm stuck in the closet."

Brown Bear wanted to rescue White Bear, but he did not know how.

Brown Bear slowly opened his
eyes and looked around.

He saw a beautiful kite above his head. Brown Bear told
White Bear what he was going to do. He had a great plan!

Brown Bear's heart beat fast as he climbed up to the kite. White Bear cheered him on. "You can do it!" said his little voice from inside the closet.

Brown Bear felt stronger now, knowing
that White Bear believed in him. He reached
for the kite and leaped out from the shelf.

He glided through the air and landed right in front of the closet.

He was still afraid, but proud to have made it. He hurried to open the closet door and climbed inside. "You are free!" he said to White Bear.

Suddenly, there was a loud thump
and the bears were in the dark.
The closet door had shut behind
Brown Bear!

Terrified, Brown Bear began to cry.
"Now we are both stuck in the closet,"
he said. "And I'm afraid of the dark too!"

White Bear patted Brown Bear's back.
"We'll be okay," he said. "We have each other."

The next morning when Alice woke up,
she didn't see Brown Bear on the shelf.
She was worried.

She went to the closet and
opened the door. There she found
White Bear and Brown Bear, sound
asleep, no longer afraid.

And Alice loved BOTH of her bears very much.